The Berenstain Bears.
AND THE
ROWDY CROWD

The Berenstain Bears.
AND THE
ROWDY CROWD

By Stan, Jan, and Mike Berenstain

ZONDERKIDZ

The Berenstain Bears and the Rowdy Crowd
Copyright © 2020 by Berenstain Publishing, LLC
Illustrations © 2020 by Berenstain Publishing, LLC

Portions of this book were previously published with the title *The Berenstain Bears The Wrong Crowd* © 2001 by Berenstain Enterprises, Inc.

Requests for information should be addressed to:
Zonderkidz, 3900 Sparks Dr. SE, Grand Rapids, Michigan 49546

Library of Congress Cataloging-in-Publication Data

Names: Berenstain, Stan, 1923–2005, author. | Berenstain, Jan, 1923–2012, author. | Berenstain, Mike, 1951-author.
Title: The Berenstain Bears and the rowdy crowd / by Stan, Jan, and Mike Berenstain.
Description: Grand Rapids, Michigan: Zonderkidz, [2020] | "Portions of this book were previously published with the title The Berenstain Bears The Wrong Crowd copyright © 2001 by Berenstain Enterprises, Inc." | Audience: Ages 6–10. | Summary: Sister is worried when Brother joins the Too-Tall gang's basketball team.
Identifiers: LCCN 2019044514 (print) | LCCN 2019044515 (ebook) | ISBN 9780310768067 (paperback) | ISBN 9780310768104 (hardcover) | ISBN 9780310768098 (epub) | ISBN 9780310768111
Subjects: CYAC: Bears—Fiction. | Brothers and sisters—Fiction. | Gangs—Fiction. | Basketball—Fiction. | Bullies—Fiction.
Classification: LCC PZ7.B4483 Bejs 2020 (print) | LCC PZ7.B4483 (ebook) | DDC [E]—dc23
LC record available at https://lccn.loc.gov/2019044514
LC ebook record available at https://lccn.loc.gov/2019044515

Art direction: Cindy Davis
Interior design: Denise Froehlich

So far, it had been a fun summer.

On most days, Sister went to the playground with her best friend, Lizzy Bruin.

They ran around the track.

They pushed each other on the swings.

They jumped rope.

There was always a third for double Dutch.

There was another good thing about the playground.

Teacher Jane was in charge. Teacher Jane was Sister's teacher. Watching the playground was her summer job.

There wasn't a lot of trouble at the playground. But there was *some.* It was mostly caused by Too-Tall and his gang.

They pushed and shoved.

They picked on younger cubs.

They threw hats into trees.

They did all the mean things bullies do.

Then one day, Too-Tall snatched Sister's best hair bow from her head.

Sister tried to grab it back. But Too-Tall was too tall!

Sister screamed and shouted, "Give me back my hair bow, you big bully!"

Too-Tall laughed down at her.

Then he threw Sister's best hair bow up into a tree.

Sister screamed and shouted some more.

That was when Brother came along.

He had been playing basketball with Cousin Fred. Brother marched up to Too-Tall.

He stood toe-to-toe with Too-Tall. His nose came up to Too-Tall's chest.

Too-Tall really *was* tall.

"Why don't you climb up and get Sister's hair bow?" said Brother.

"Yeah?" said too-Tall. "What are you gonna do to me if I don't?"

Too-Tall stood nose-to-nose with Brother. He had to bend down to do it. It was scary how big he was.

But Brother stood his ground.

"If you don't—" began Brother.

That was when Teacher Jane came over.

"What seems to be the problem?" she asked.

Sister said, "Too-Tall threw my best hair bow into the tree."

"I just asked him to climb up and get it down," added Brother.

"That sounds like a good idea to me," said Teacher Jane to Too-Tall. "And after you've done that, I'd like you and your gang to please leave the playground. Bullies aren't welcome here."

Too-Tall grumbled. But he climbed up the tree. He got the hair bow. He gave it back to Sister.

Then he took his gang and left.

"Thanks, Brother," said Sister.

But Brother was staring off after Too-Tall and his gang.

At the playground a few days later, Brother was by himself shooting free throws. There was a buzz.

The Too-Tall gang was back again.

They headed right for the court.

Skuzz caught the ball and bounced it hard.

"This court's ours now," said Skuzz. "Get lost."

But then something strange happened.

"Leave him alone," said Too-Tall.
"What?" Skuzz said.
"I said leave him alone."
"Sure thing, boss."

Skuzz and the rest of the gang backed off.

Brother stared at Too-Tall. Was the big guy trying to make friends?

Brother wondered why big, scary Too-Tall would want to be friends with a goody-goody like himself.

Was it because he had stood up to him the other day?

The next minute, Brother found out why.

"I've been watching you play this summer," said Too-Tall. "You've got the makings of a pretty good point guard."

Brother couldn't believe what he was hearing. Too-Tall thought he was good?

Too-Tall went on. "Want to play some *real* basketball? Forget about this baby playground. Play with us. We've got a team of our own. Our court is in the woods behind the junkyard. Meet you there in an hour."

Brother felt ten feet tall.

"Okay!" he said.

He couldn't believe he had said yes. What if his parents found out? They'd ground him forever.

Everybody knew about the Too-Tall gang.

Everybody knew they were bad.

They were always in trouble at school.

They had even been kicked out a couple of times.

Brother wasn't sure why. But

it must have been something pretty bad.

Someone said that it was for fighting.

Someone else said that it was for stealing.

But Brother wasn't going to get mixed up with the Too-Tall gang. He was just going to play a little basketball with them. What harm could there be in that?

Brother knew they were a bad bunch. But he couldn't help feeling proud.

He wondered what it would be like to be part of the Too-Tall gang. He wondered what it would be like to have other cubs be scared of you and step aside when you came along.

Mostly, he wondered what it would be like to play on their court in the woods.

He didn't have to wait long to find out.

Brother Bear made his way past the junkyard toward the woods. The woods were just ahead. Next to the path, there was a wooden sign stuck in the ground.

It said: KEEP OUT! THIS MEANS YOU!

There was a skull and bones on the sign.

But Brother had an invitation from Too-Tall himself, so it was all right. At least that's what he kept telling himself.

Brother took a deep breath and went into the woods.

There was no sign of life— except for plant life, of course. And there was plenty of that. The trees were all tangled with twisty vines. It was pretty spooky.

He looked up into the trees.

Things were hanging from the branches. He couldn't tell what they were.

It looked as if the woods might go on forever. Then he came to a clearing. There was a basketball court. It had a dirt floor. There were baskets bolted to trees at each end of the court.

There was a small building at the far end of the clearing. It was made out of pieces of junk.

Since the junkyard was close by, that made sense.

Smoke was coming out of the chimney. The chimney looked like a truck's tailpipe. Now that Brother looked closely, the whole clubhouse was made from car and truck parts.

What a great setup! A whole basketball court and a clubhouse made out of car and truck parts.

But where *was* everybody?

There was a basketball lying on the court.

Brother picked it up. He started to dribble down the court.

Just then, the gang poured out of the clubhouse.

But where was Too-Tall?

The gang didn't look friendly. Brother had gotten them kicked off the playground. They were probably still angry about it.

"Where's Too-Tall?" asked Brother.

"*We* ask the questions around here," said Skuzz.

They backed Brother up against a tree.

"And the first question is, didn't

you see the sign that says 'Keep out! This means you!'?"

Brother didn't answer.

If Too-Tall didn't show up soon, he was in deep trouble.

"Maybe he can't read," said Skuzz.

"Maybe he doesn't like signs," said Vinnie.

"Do you want to know what we do to cubs who don't like signs?" said Smirk.

Brother didn't answer.

"If you want to know," said Skuzz, "just look up in the trees."

Brother looked up.

Now he got it.

Those things in the trees were pants. There were all kinds—long pants, short pants, and jeans.

"That's right," said Vinnie. "We 'pants' cubs who don't like signs. We send them home crying—in their underwear."

Brother looked around for Too-Tall.

There was still no sign of him. Brother knew he had to make his move before the gang made theirs.

He threw the basketball at them as hard as he could. It knocked Skuzz down. He pulled Vinnie and Smirk down with him.

Brother was off like a shot. He ran along the path as fast as he could.

The gang was hot on his heels. He was almost out of the woods when he ran smack into Too-Tall.

"Oof!" grunted Too-Tall. "What's going on?"

Brother started to say. But Too-Tall got it, all right.

He was very mad. He grabbed Skuzz by the shirt.

"You let Brother alone!" he yelled. "I want him on our team! And what I say goes! Got it?"

"G-g-g-got it," said Skuzz. Vinnie and Smirk nodded.

"Now go get our team shirts," said Too-Tall. "We're playing the Westside Thugs today."

The game between the Westside Thugs and the Junkyard Dogs was fast and hard. A big teenage ref called a lot of fouls. Even so, the game was hard.

Too-Tall was right about Brother. He was a very good point guard. The team played well. Brother played very well. But the Junkyard Dogs still lost.

Skuzz, Vinnie, and Smirk were

out of breath. They lay down on the grass.

Too-Tall had gotten into a fight with the captain of the Westside Thugs, who was even taller than Too-Tall.

But now that the game was over, they were talking about playing each other again.

Too-Tall was out of breath too. He sat down on the grass. Too-Tall was not a good loser. But Brother had something to tell him.

"Too-Tall?" said Brother.

"Yeah," grunted Too-Tall.

"I have something to tell you," he said. "If you play the Westside

Thugs again, you're just going to lose again."

"Who *says* so?" snarled Too-Tall.

"It's just good sense," said Brother. "You've got no bench. You can't play big-time basketball with just five players. The Thugs are a good team. And they've got a bench. They can send in players with fresh legs. You need at least a sixth player to come off the bench."

"So what do we do?" sneered Too-Tall.

"I could talk to my cousin," said Brother.

"You don't mean that little twerp from the playground?" said Too-Tall.

"You've got to be kidding!" added Skuzz.

"Fred may be small," said Brother, "but he's no twerp. He's a good player. He's fast and he can run all day. He's a good bench player."

"Do you think he'll be interested?" asked Too-Tall.

"I can ask him," said Brother.

"Now, just a darn minute!" said Skuzz. He got up off the ground. Vinnie and Smirk got up too.

"You got a problem with that?" asked Too-Tall.

"Yeah!" said Skuzz. "Why does *he* have a say in what we do? This is gang biz! And he's not even in the gang!"

"He has a say because I *say* he has a say!" roared Too-Tall. "Unless you're looking for a knuckle sandwich, back off!"

Skuzz backed off. He backed off so fast he knocked Vinnie and Smirk down.

"Okay, Brother," said Too-Tall. "Ask your cousin. I'll let you know when the next game is."

Then Too-Tall and the gang got up. They went back into their clubhouse. They left Brother outside. He shrugged and got up to go home.

Brother came out of the woods into the bright sunlight. His feet hardly seemed to touch the ground. What a feeling! What a kick! He had played well in a big-time basketball game. Plus, big, bad Too-Tall was taking his advice.

He walked past the junkyard.

He thought about the gang's great clubhouse. It didn't take much to figure out where the gang got the car parts. They stole them from the junkyard. But was that *really* stealing? It was just junk. And it was such a cool clubhouse.

As Brother walked along, he leaned forward and bent his knees.

If he was going to hang out with tough guys, he figured he might as well have a tough walk too.

That night, Sister lay in bed.

She was wondering what was up with Brother. It wasn't that Brother was being mean. It was just that lately he seemed far away—even when she was standing next to him. When she asked him something, all she got was "Huh?"

Not that they always agreed. After all, Brother was older than she was. Not only that, Brother was a boy and she was a girl. But that was nothing new. What was new was that Brother didn't seem the same.

Sister liked having her own room. She liked it a lot. She liked not tripping over Brother's toys. She liked not having Brother's sports things all over the place. She liked not having to smell his awful model airplane glue.

Sister guessed that Brother liked having his own room too—a room free of dolls, stuffed toys, and all her girl things.

But she lay looking up into the shadows.

She listened to the *tick-tock* of the pussycat clock on the wall.

It was the kind with eyes and a tail that go from side-to-side with each *tick-tock*.

Why was it that things seemed a little spooky before you fell asleep?

Things looked different when Sister woke up the next morning.

Things *usually* look different in the morning.

It was the same room, but it was bright with rays of the rising sun. It was the same pussycat clock on the wall. But by the light of day, it seemed cheerful.

Sister washed and dressed for breakfast. She tried to shrug off her worries about Brother.

Yes, said Sister to herself, *things surely do look different in the morning.* She bounced down the tree house stairs and into the kitchen.

Breakfast was a cheerful time in the tree house. In summer, there wasn't the rush-rush of catching the school bus. She and Lizzy Bruin had the whole day ahead of them at the playground.

Thinking of the playground reminded Sister of how Brother had stood up to Too-Tall for her. She felt a wave of warm feelings about him. She forgot all about how he had changed.

"Brother," she said. "I don't know

if you have any plans for today. But how about the two of us doing something together?"

Brother didn't answer. He just stared straight ahead.

"I *said*," said Sister, much louder, "do you have any plans for today? Maybe we could do something together."

Still no answer from Brother.

"Brother," said Mama, "your sister just asked you something."

Brother turned and looked at Sister. It was as if he had never seen her before.

"Huh?" he said.

"I said . . . oh, never mind," said

Sister. She poured herself some cereal and milk.

If it was a bad mood, thought Sister, it sure was a long one. *Okay, if he's such a big shot he can't talk to his own sister, who needs him?*

She dug into her cereal. She crunched down hard.

"What *are* your plans for today?" Mama asked Brother.

"Oh, er, I'm going to shoot some hoops with Cousin Fred," said Brother.

"Shoot some hoops?" said Mama.

"That means 'play basketball,'" said Sister.

"I see," said Mama. She turned

41

to Brother. "Is that right, Brother?" she asked.

But Brother was gone. He had left the table and was out the door and down the road.

So all Sister's worries about Brother weren't just night thoughts. Something was going on with Brother. He had changed.

She turned to Papa, who was reading his paper.

"Papa," she said, "I'm sure you've noticed that something is going on with Brother. What do you think it could be?"

Papa didn't answer. He just kept on reading his paper.

"Papa," said Sister much louder. "I'm *sure* you've seen that something is going on with Brother. What do you think it could be?" Papa put down his paper and looked at Sister.

"Huh?" he said.

Sister gave up on Papa and headed for the playground.

Her mind was still on Brother. *If he wants to be snooty, let him be snooty. But two can play the snooty game. Just wait till the next time he asks me to play checkers or catch fly balls for him. I'll just give him the same blank look he gives me and say, "Huh?"*

Just then, she met Cousin Fred coming the other way. He was carrying a fishing pole.

"Hi, Fred," said Sister. "Where are you headed?"

"*Your* house," said Fred. "I thought I'd pick up Brother and we could do some fishing."

"He's not there," said Sister. "He said he was going to shoot some hoops with *you*."

"That's the first I've heard about it," said Fred. "But maybe I'm mixed up."

But Sister didn't think Fred was mixed up.

Sister thought Brother was just

lying about playing basketball with Cousin Fred.

If Brother wasn't playing basketball, what was he doing?

Now Sister knew for sure. Something was up with Brother.

And she had a feeling that the *Something* had something to do with Too-Tall.

Fred had his own backyard basket. He was shooting free throws later that day when Brother came by.

Fred was a very good free throw shooter. But he missed the basket when Brother mentioned Too-Tall. The ball bounced into the bushes.

"Join the Too-Tall team? You and me?" said Fred. "Are you out of your mind? They're the worst! How can you even *think* of getting mixed up with the Too-Tall gang?"

Brother just smiled. He got the ball out of the bushes and started dribbling it toward the basket.

"Okay, Fred," he said. "Let's see if you can stop my best move."

"No problem," said Fred.

Brother was very fast. But Fred was fast too. As Brother made his move, Fred reached in, stole the ball, and laid it up.

"Way to go!" said Brother. He put his arm around Fred. "See what I mean? We'll make a great backcourt."

"You really think so?" said Fred. He was proud.

"I *know* so," said Brother.

"Yeah," said Fred. "But the whole

idea of getting mixed up with the Too-Tall gang worries me."

"We're not going to get *mixed up* with them! We're just going to play a little basketball with them."

"Gee, I don't know," said Fred.

Brother picked up the basketball. He shot the ball. Swish! He got nothing but net.

"Of course," said Brother, "if you're too chicken to play some real basketball . . ."

He started to walk away.

"I'm not chicken!" said Fred. He hurried to catch up with Brother.

Soon Fred and Brother were walking along Junkyard Road.

"You know," said Brother, "we're going to have to keep this all a secret."

"You've got that right," said Fred. "What will we tell our parents?"

"Let's just say that we've joined a new team. It's the truth."

But Fred was still scared about joining the Too-Tall team. He got even more scared when he saw the KEEP OUT! sign.

"Don't be scared," said Brother. "I'm here to protect you."

"Yeah," said Fred. "But who's going to protect *you*?"

"Too-Tall," said Brother. "We're buddies. We're like this." Brother

held out his hand and crossed his middle finger over his index finger. "That's how close we are."

"Maybe so," said Fred. "But you know what they say: 'He who lies down with dogs gets up with fleas.'"

"Well, there are no fleas on me," Brother said.

He took Fred by the arm and pulled him into the woods.

"What are those pants hanging in the trees?" asked Fred.

Brother did not tell Fred about the pants. Fred was scared enough as it was.

Fred not only made the team, he ran circles around Skuzz, Vinnie, and Smirk. They didn't like it. But Too-Tall did. With Brother as his star point guard and Fred coming off the bench, maybe they could beat the Westside Thugs.

"Okay, you two," Too-Tall said. "The game's tomorrow. Be here!"

Fred was quiet as they walked back along Junkyard Road.

"You really looked good back there," said Brother.

"Thanks," said Fred.

But he was still worried.

"Will you *please* stop worrying? Look at it this way," said Brother. "Playing with Too-Tall could really improve our game. We might even make the school team next year."

"Or you could look at it this way," said Fred. "If we don't win, they could steal our pants and send us home in our underwear."

So Fred knew what the pants were about.

"And speaking of underwear," said Fred, "why are you walking

funny? Are your shorts caught?"

"I'm not walking funny," said
Brother. "That's the way I walk."

"Oh," said Fred.

It was Arts and Crafts Day at the playground.

Sister and Lizzy had signed up for the flower vase project. The idea was to make a beautiful vase out of a jar. Teacher Jane said it had to be a clean jar.

Sister brought in a pickle jar.

Lizzy brought in a jelly jar.

Getting the pickle smell out of the pickle jar wasn't easy. It took a lot of hot water. But now it was clean, and Sister was pressing clay onto it.

Lizzy was doing the same thing. After the clay dried, they would paint the vases. Lizzy was planning to dent the clay all over with her fingers. Then she would paint each dent a different color.

Sister had another idea. She planned on orange and black stripes like a tiger's. Mama grew tiger lilies in her garden. Now Mama would have a special vase for her tiger lilies.

Sister was smoothing out the clay on her vase when Brother and Fred came by. They were headed for the basketball court. They didn't even stop to say hello.

"You hold the court, Fred," said Brother. "I'll go into the office and sign out the ball. The big game's tomorrow and we have to practice."

Sister watched Brother head for the office. He had begun to walk funny lately.

She had seen that walk somewhere before.

Where had she seen it?

"Oh, Fred," she said, "I don't know if you know, but something weird is going on with Brother. Does it have anything to do with basketball?"

Fred didn't answer.

Sister reached out and tapped him on the shoulder. "Fred, I just asked you something."

Fred turned and looked at her.

"Huh?" he said.

"I *said* I just asked you something!"

But Fred was gone. There was no "Excuse me," or "See you later." He just left Sister standing there with her face hanging out.

Sister watched them practice their moves. But she sensed that there was more going on than basketball.

She thought back to when it all

started. It was the day Too-Tall threw her hair bow into a tree.

No, it was a few days after that, when the Too-Tall gang tried to push Brother off the basketball court. She could see Too-Tall in her mind's eye. She could see that tough walk of his.

But wait! That was it! *That's* where Brother got that walk! Which could mean only one thing. Brother was mixed up with the bad, nasty, low-down Too-Tall gang!

As Sister lay in her bed that night, she was back to worrying about Brother.

She worried about how he had changed.

She worried about his new tough walk.

Mostly, she worried about him hanging around with Too-Tall.

She didn't know for sure he was hanging around with Too-Tall. She had to find out. But how?

Just before she fell asleep, she got an idea. It might be danger-ous. But then, anything that had to do with Too-Tall was dangerous. Dangerous or not, she would do it in the morning.

Sister kept a notebook. That night she wrote in it:

Brother still acting like a jerk. Going to find out about it tomorrow.

Sister was the last to come down to breakfast. Brother was spooning up his cereal like there was no tomorrow.

"Brother," said Mama, "would you

please stop gobbling your breakfast? It's not healthy."

"Yesh, ma'am," said Brother.

"And please don't speak with
your mouth full," added Mama.

"What's the big hurry, son?" asked Papa.

"Going to play some basketball," said Brother. "Fred and I have joined a new team."

Yeah, thought Sister, *the Too-Tall team.*

"Well, gotta go," said Brother. He pushed away from the table and was out the door.

Sister finished her breakfast. Then she left and put her plan into action.

Sister's plan was simple: follow Brother and find out just what was going on with him.

Keeping out of sight, she followed

Brother to Fred's house. Then she followed the two of them along Junkyard Road. As she sneaked along behind them, she could see that Fred was hanging back. But Brother urged him on.

As she followed them into the woods, she heard voices. She moved from tree to tree. Then she hid in the bushes beside the basketball court and watched the game.

It was the second game between the Westside Thugs and the Junkyard Dogs. It went down to the wire. The Dogs were down by two points, with seconds to go. The Thugs were double-teaming

Too-Tall. That left Brother open. He was at the three-point line. Too-Tall passed him the ball.

Brother shot. *Swish!* Nothing but net!

The Junkyard Dogs won by one point. A cheer went up. Fred had played well coming off the bench. But Brother had been the star of the game. The gang crowded around him. Too-Tall put his hand out.

"Let me shake the hand of the newest member of the Too-Tall gang."

"Huh?" said Brother. He looked shocked down to his toes. So did Cousin Fred.

"Well, good game, guys," said Fred. "See you later. Gotta get home."

"Wait!" said Brother. "We won. Don't you want to hang around?"

"We don't need that twerp," said Too-Tall. "Let him go."

Sister was shocked. How could Brother even *think* of joining the Too-Tall gang? They were the worst.

They pushed and shoved.

They threw hats (and hair bows) into trees.

They even made little cubs cry.

But what to do? She could go home and tell Mama and Papa. But that would be tattling. Besides, all Brother had done was play basketball.

At least, so far.

"Come on," said Too-Tall.

"Where are we going?" asked Brother.

"To our secret stash," said Too-Tall with a big grin.

"What's *that*?" asked Brother.

"It's where we keep our stuff," said Skuzz.

"What stuff is that?" asked Brother.

"Button it up, Skuzz!" ordered Too-Tall. "We don't want to give away the whole show."

Good grief! They were headed straight for Sister! She scrunched down behind the bushes. They went right by. Phew!

"Come on, shake a leg," said Too-Tall. "We got things to do."

"What things?" asked Brother. He sounded a little nervous.

"You gotta get initiated, for one thing," said Vinnie.

"Initiated?" said Brother.

"Sure," said Smirk. "You don't expect to get into the Too-Tall gang without gettin' initiated."

"Er, what am I going to have to do?" asked Brother. Now he looked very nervous.

"You'll see," said Skuzz with a nasty chuckle.

Sister followed as close as she dared.

What *was* Brother going to have to do?

Be rude to old ladies?

Push little cubs around?

Cheat and tell lies?

But there was no turning back

now. She followed the Too-Tall gang and its newest member deeper and deeper into the woods.

Sister dared not get too close. Who would be madder if she got caught? Brother or the Too-Tall gang?

The woods got thicker. The gang walked past a big sign that said: Mr. Grizzwold's Land. NO TRESPASSING. Skuzz kicked the sign. Too-Tall laughed. Sister snuck past the sign.

Mr. Grizzwold was grumpy. He had big dogs. He did not like tres-passers. Come to think of it, he didn't like most folks. Thornbushes seemed to reach out and grab Sister. Burs snagged her clothes.

After a hard climb up a steep hill, they came to a hollow.

Down in the hollow was what was left of a stone building. It looked like a springhouse, a small storehouse built over a brook.

Gramps and Gran had a springhouse. But this one was a ruin.

The Too-Tall gang walked up to a big hole in the wall. Brother stopped.

"Come on," said Too-Tall. "Our stash is in here." Brother didn't move.

"Mr. Grizzwold doesn't like cubs messing around here," said Brother.

"That's because it's haunted," said Skuzz.

The springhouse looked haunted. Big, dark shadows spread out in the corners. Stringy cobwebs hung all over. The roof and the walls were falling apart. Sister hoped they wouldn't fall apart on top of Brother.

"Mr. Grizzwold calls the police on trespassers," said Brother. "If we get caught, we could get in a lot of trouble."

"Are you scared of a little ghost?" said Skuzz. He had a big, mean grin.

Too-Tall crossed his arms. "I don't want any little scaredy-cats on my team or in my gang," Too-Tall said. "You have to go in the haunted springhouse for an hour to be initiated. If you are too scared, we'll put your pants in a tree! Just like the other scaredy-cat cubs!"

"I'm not scared," said Brother. He crawled into the hole. Skuzz and Too-Tall crawled in after him.

Sister could hear voices inside the springhouse, but she couldn't see anything.

She had to get closer. But how to do it without getting caught?

There was a bent-over tree next to the ruin. Ever so quietly and ever so carefully, she climbed the tree.

She inched her way along a big branch until she could see. She could hardly believe her eyes. Sister could see piles of candy and comic books. She didn't know where the Too-Tall gang got their stash. But she knew they probably didn't pay for it.

"Where did you guys get all this?" asked Brother.

"Around town," said Skuzz. "You're not gonna tattle, are you, Brother?"

"N-n-no," said Brother.

"Then take some," said Too-Tall, and he handed Brother a big chocolate candy bar.

Sister shifted for a better look.

There was Brother in Mr. Grizzwold's springhouse, eating stolen candy!

Suddenly, Sister heard a loud CREAK! Brother and the Too-Tall gang heard it too. They all jumped up.

"It's the ghost!" shouted Skuzz.

Sister couldn't stay there.

She had to get home.

She inched back down the bent-over tree.

Upset and almost crying, she ran back through the woods as fast as she could.

The woods fought her all the way.

Rocks tripped her.

Brambles scratched her.

Branches tore at her clothes.

She fell and skinned her knees.

She slipped and rolled down hills. But she kept going. She had to get home.

But what was she going to do when she got there? All her life, she had been told not to tattle. And who would believe her anyway?

Who would believe that goody-goody Brother had joined the Too-Tall gang? Who would believe he was trespassing and eating stolen candy?

By the time she got home, she was a mess. Her face was scratched. Her clothes were torn. Her hair bow was hanging loose.

Mama and Papa heard her coming up the front steps. Sister came in the door. Mama and Papa gasped.

"My goodness!" said Mama. "What happened to you?"

"Where have you *been*?" said Papa.

Sister sat down and began to cry. "I—I—I can't tell you!" she sobbed.

Mama sat beside her and hugged her.

"Of course you can, my dear," said Mama.

"I—I—I can't," sobbed Sister. "It's—it's—it's too awful!"

"Did somebody hurt you?" asked Papa.

Sister shook her head. Sobs shook her little body.

"Now, now," said Mama, leaning in close.

"Let us help, Sister," said Papa. "We can't help if we don't know what happened. Is something wrong with Brother?"

That did it. Sister blurted out the whole story: about Brother joining the Too-Tall gang, about the initiation in the springhouse, and about the ghost.

"Well, I'll be!" said Papa, looking like a storm cloud.

"Please calm down, my dear," said Mama. "I'm sure we can deal with this."

Sister was still sobbing.

"Please stop crying, sweetheart. You were right to tell us," said Mama. "And there is no such thing as a ghost or a haunted springhouse. There is such a thing as a dangerous springhouse. Cubs can get hurt messing around in broken-down buildings. Now that we know where Brother is, we can help him."

"B-B-Brother's gonna hate me for tattling," said Sister.

"That'll be *his* problem," said Papa. "Telling something to help someone you love is not tattling. Tell me, Sister, do you think you can find this springhouse again?"

"Sure," said Sister.

"What are you going to do?" asked Mama.

"Sister and I are going to save that scamp from that nasty gang!"

"Oh, boy!" said Sister.

But they didn't get very far. As they started down the front steps, Chief of Police Bruno drove up in the police car.

The chief got out. He went around to the passenger side. He opened the door. Guess who got out?

It was Brother. It was a sad-looking, sick-looking Brother.

"What's this about, Chief?" asked Papa.

"It's about a cub getting mixed up with the wrong crowd," said the chief. "That's the wrong crowd in the *back* of the police car."

And sure enough, there was the Too-Tall gang in the backseat trying to look small.

"Brother, you march yourself into the house," said Papa.

They watched as Brother slowly climbed the front steps and went into the house.

"I understand you must have caught them in Mr. Grizzwold's old springhouse, Chief," said Papa. "Sister told us all about it."

"Good for her," said the chief. "That wasn't the worst of it. The Too-Tall gang's been breaking into vending machines. Stole tons of soda and candy. They were taking other stuff too. We finally found their hideout and nailed them with the goods. Well, I've got to take them in."

"What will happen to the gang, Chief?" asked Papa.

The chief shrugged. "That'll be up to Judge Gavel. Er, one other thing—I'd speak to your lad about hanging out with the wrong crowd. Next time, *he* might be the one caught stealing. Besides that, that old springhouse could fall down at any time. The cubs might have gotten hurt."

"Count on it," said Papa. "And thanks."

Sister watched as the police car drove away.

She wondered what was going to happen to the Too-Tall gang. She also wondered what was going to happen to Brother.

Back in the house, Papa was pacing.

Brother looked very small in the big easy chair.

"Well, young fellow," said Papa, "what do you have to say for yourself?"

"I don't know what to say," said Brother.

"Well, for starters," said Papa, "you could say you will never have anything to do with the Too-Tall gang again. And that you'll never, ever, ever, *ever* go onto someone else's property without permission again."

"I never will," said Brother. "That goes for both the gang and the trespassing."

"And," added Papa, "you could thank your sister, who was worried sick about you."

"He doesn't have to thank me," said Sister.

"Yes, I do," said Brother. "I was acting dumb and you knew it."

"Brother," said Mama, "do you have any idea how dangerous that springhouse is? Mr. Grizzwold has rules for a reason."

"Sort of, I guess," said Brother.

"Well, just to make sure," said Mama, "we're going to go to Mr. Grizzwold's house and you are going to apologize to him in person for not respecting his land and his rules."

"Do we *have* to talk to Mr. Grizzwold?" asked Brother.

"Yes, we have to," said Mama.

Sister went over to Brother.

"Brother," she said.

"Yes," said Brother.

"Do you have any plans for tomorrow?" she said. "Maybe we can do something together."

"Sounds good," said Brother.

That night, Sister decided it was time to write something in her notebook again. This is what she wrote:

And she did.

The Berenstain Bears' Nature Rescue

An Early Reader Chapter Book

Stan, Jan, and Mike Berenstain

Save the birds! Save the trees! That's what the cubs are saying around Bear Country. If Squire Grizzly gets his way and cuts down the trees in Birder's Woods, the yellow popinjays will have nowhere to rest. They could disappear forever. It's up to the cubs to save this important part of nature before it's too late!

The Berenstain Bears' Nature Rescue is an engaging early reader chapter book that features black and white illustrations alongside entertaining text and relatable characters. As read-alone or read-aloud, it helps kids connect plot to chapter structure and will have teachers and librarians asking for more. And as part of the beloved Living Lights: A Faith Story series, it's the perfect segue for emerging readers and fans of the Berenstain brand.

When kids graduate from picture books to chapter books, it's a great moment. Mama, Papa, Brother, Sister, and Honey will captivate readers ages 6–10 who are ready to take the next step in their reading comprehension.

Available in stores and online!

The Berenstain Bears' Epic Dog Show

An Early Reader Chapter Book

Stan, Jan, and Mike Berenstain

Brother and Sister Bear may have come up with their greatest idea yet: a super-duper dog show to be held at the Beartown church fair. Dogs large and small will do amazing tricks, and Dr. Hairball, the vet, will judge. The Arfo Dog Biscuit Company has even agreed to give out prizes to each and every dog. It's sure to be the best dog show ever, or is it? Find out what happens when Too-Tall and the gang decide to crash the big show.

The Berenstain Bears' Epic Dog Show is an engaging early reader chapter book that features black and white illustrations alongside entertaining text and relatable characters. As read-alone or read-aloud, it helps kids connect plot to chapter structure and will have teachers and librarians asking for more. And as part of the beloved Living Lights: A Faith Story series, it's the perfect segue for emerging readers and fans of the Berenstain brand.

When kids graduate from picture books to chapter books, it's a great moment. Mama, Papa, Brother, Sister, and Honey will captivate readers ages 6–10 who are ready to take the next step in their reading comprehension.

Available in stores and online!

The Berenstain Bears' The Trouble with Tryouts

An Early Reader Chapter Book

Stan, Jan, and Mike Berenstain

Sister Bear is a super soccer player. She's fast on her feet. She kicks the ball with the power of a cub twice her size. She should be a shoo-in at soccer tryouts; except for one little problem. Sister Bear is too small. Even Mama, Papa, and Brother think Sister has set her sights too high. Will Sister make the team despite her size? Or will she be stuck on the sidelines?

The Berenstain Bears The Trouble with Tryouts is an engaging early reader chapter book that features black and white illustrations alongside entertaining text and relatable characters. As read-alone or read-aloud, it helps kids connect plot to chapter structure and will have teachers and librarians asking for more. And as part of the beloved Living Lights: A Faith Story series, it's the perfect segue for emerging readers and fans of the Berenstain brand.

When kids graduate from picture books to chapter books, it's a great moment. Mama, Papa, Brother, Sister, and Honey will captivate readers ages 6-10 who are ready to take the next step in their reading comprehension.

Available in stores and online!